UNDERWORLDS

THE ICE DRAGON

TO MODERN
HEROES,
WHEREVER
YOU ARE

No part of this publication may be reproduced, stored in a retrieval system, or transmitted in any form or by any means, electronic, mechanical, photocopying, recording, or otherwise, without written permission of the publisher. For information regarding permission, write to Scholastic Inc., Attention: Permissions Department, 557 Broadway, New York, NY 10012.

ISBN 978-0-545-30834-2

Text copyright © 2012 by Robert T. Abbott

Illustrations copyright © 2012 by Scholastic Inc.

All rights reserved. Published by Scholastic Inc.

SCHOLASTIC and associated logos are trademarks
and/or registered trademarks of Scholastic Inc.

12 11 10 9 8 7 6 5 4 3 2 1   12 13 14 15 16 17/0

Printed in the U.S.A.   40
First printing, December 2012
DESIGNED BY YAFFA JASKOLL

UNDERWORLDS

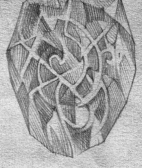

BOOK FOUR

THE ICE DRAGON

BY **TONY ABBOTT**

ILLUSTRATED BY

ANTONIO JAVIER CAPARO

Scholastic Inc.

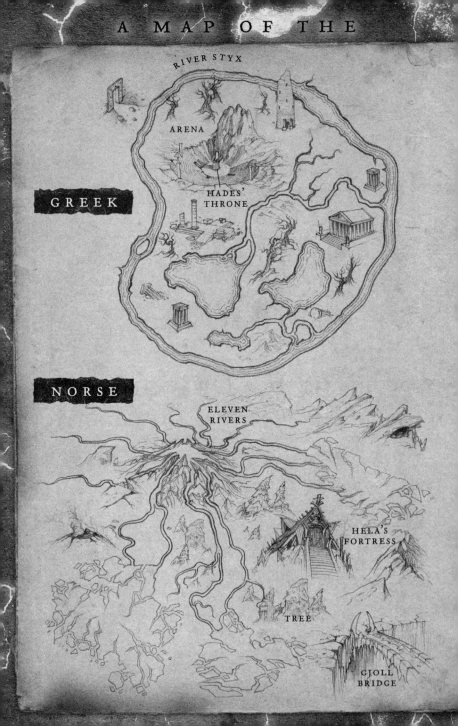

RIVER STYX

ARENA

GREEK

HADES'
THRONE

NORSE

ELEVEN
RIVERS

HELA'S
FORTRESS

TREE

GJOLL
BRIDGE

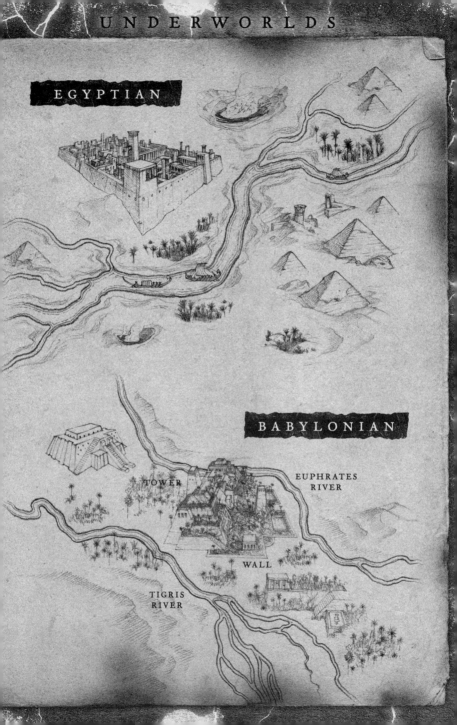

EGYPTIAN

BABYLONIAN

TOWER

EUPHRATES
RIVER

WALL

TIGRIS
RIVER

CHAPTER ONE

INTO THE
NORTHERN NIGHT

MY NAME IS OWEN BROWN.

Normally, I live in Pinewood Bluffs with my friends Jon Doyle, Dana Runson, and Sydney Lamberti. But normal wasn't normal anymore, and hadn't been for weeks. Take right now, for example. We were clinging to giant mythical horses, flying a hundred miles an hour across the freezing skies to Iceland.

Iceland!

And since we'd never been encased in ancient Norse war armor or ridden flying horses, we didn't know that cold wind whistles into iron helmets and freezes your eyeballs.

But we were finding out.

"Stopppppp!" I screamed.

"No time!" shouted Miss Hilda, the armor-clad lady flying ahead of us. In her mythological life, Miss Hilda was Doom Rider, one of the famous Valkyries from Norse mythology. They were the three daughters of the supreme Norse god, Odin, and they chose which heroes died in battle. So far, they hadn't chosen us.

Oh, yeah — in their other lives, the Valkyries were the lunch ladies at Pinewood Bluffs Elementary.

"Look there!" said Miss Marge through her silver helmet, pointing to the earth below.

Blinking the icicles from our eyes, we saw a white island in a frozen sea.

"Iceland!" said the third warrior lady, Miss Lillian. "Land of the Norse gods!"

The Valkyries sang their favorite tagline — "Hoyo-Toho!" — and all seven horses dove like missiles seeking a target. Hanging on for dear life, my eyes shut as tight as I could make them, my mind spun with the events of the last few days. They weren't pretty.

First, the evil Norse god Loki stole Dana away to the Greek Underworld. Then Sydney, Jon, and I snatched the famous Lyre of Orpheus from a museum and rescued Dana. Next, Loki brought the giant, one-eyed Cyclopes to the power plant in Pinewood Bluffs to make him a suit of magic armor. Once his armor was complete, he stole a half-dozen fire monsters from the Babylonian Underworld and set them loose to burn up our planet. Oh, and then he turned around and had Dana's parents kidnapped, sent them to the Norse Underworld, and started searching for something called the Crystal Rune.

All so he could overthrow Odin and take power for himself.

Miss Marge's booming voice cut through my thoughts. "Odin's messengers approach. We fly to them!"

As the Valkyries urged their giant horses to fly faster, the air echoed with a long, eerie call. Two ravens —

one white, one black — circled out of the sky and joined us.

"What news do you bring us?" Miss Hilda asked the birds.

The ravens fluttered alongside her, chattering and clacking their beaks. A moment later, they flew back into the clouds.

"Loki has left the Babylonian fire monsters to complete their task in Pinewood Bluffs and beyond," said Miss Lillian. "He has come here to the north. Alone."

"This is good, right?" said Jon. "I mean, not the fire monsters part, but the fact that Loki's still up here?"

It was good. Ever since Loki's ghostly Draug warriors had kidnapped Dana's parents, Dana had worried about her parents being trapped in the Norse land of the dead, a creepy place called Niflheim. The upside was that the Crystal Rune was still in our world somewhere — and apparently, only Dana knew where. So Loki wasn't about to harm Dana's parents. He needed them as leverage.

At least we hoped so.

"We need to find the Crystal Rune as fast as we can," said Sydney. "Those fire monsters will burn our world to ash."

The horses leaped forward, making a beeline for the coast of Iceland.

"There's an old legend about the Crystal Rune being buried near the island's northernmost volcano," Dana said. "We'll only be able to bargain with Loki if we have the rune."

So we knew what we had to do.

Find the Crystal Rune.

Stop Loki.

Rescue Dana's parents.

Oh. And stay alive, too.

That was a big one.

Just as we began to make out the shape of Iceland's mountains below, the air fluttered behind us.

"More birds from Odin?" asked Jon.

"No!" cried Miss Hilda. "Ghost falcons! Dive! Dive!"

The Valkyries slapped the reins and drove their horses downward. Ours followed. I wasn't sure whether the ghost falcons spotted us, but they kept flying due north — exactly where we were heading.

"Loki's falcons will join the battle for Odin's throne," Miss Lillian said ominously from behind her helmet. "Their appearance means that Ragnarok is near."

Ragnarok is a word in ancient Norse that means *the end.* The Twilight of the Gods. The end of the world of Norse divinity. I couldn't imagine what that might look like, but I knew it was bad.

"That's two signs," said Dana. "The Fires of Midgard are one of the signs predicted before the overthrow of Odin, too. We just saw that happen — all of Pinewood Bluffs was on fire. Loki's making sure all the predictions happen."

We dipped out of the clouds over a vast body of frozen water. It looked like a lake, but it was actually the opening of a humongous volcano, miles across.

"The legend tells us that the Crystal Rune was hidden by Odin himself," Dana said as we circled overhead. "But there was one book that revealed that the rune was in the crater of the northernmost volcano in Iceland, 'buried by sound and silence.' My parents burned the book to keep it from Loki, but they read it to me over and over. I guess they knew I'd need to find the rune someday."

Dana drew in a long breath. I couldn't imagine how worried she was about her parents. If my family was in the Underworld, I'd spare nothing to get them back.

Tiny villages clustered on the south side of the volcano below were dwarfed by the enormity of the crater. Soon the horses landed at a fast gallop on the rim.

"*Buried by sound and silence*," Sydney repeated. "It figures there would be a riddle attached. Nothing ever comes easy when the end of the world is at stake."

"I hope we don't get buried there ourselves," said Jon. Silence. He added, "Don't everyone laugh at once."

We dismounted. Together, Sydney and I helped the Valkyries hammer an iron post into the edge of the rim, attach a thick rope to it, and lower the rope down the inside wall of the crater.

"This volcano is extinct, right?" asked Sydney.

"Usually," said Miss Marge.

"Usually?" said Jon. "What should we do if it starts to get active again?"

Miss Hilda peered into the crater. Without a hint of humor, she said, "Remember the good times."

Sydney blinked. "All ten years of them."

"Take these torches," Miss Lillian said, unpacking two sticks from her horse's saddlebag and lighting them. "We must go. Odin needs us. Good luck."

"Wait," said Jon. "Any other words of advice before you go?"

Miss Marge looked sternly down from her horse. "Always remember . . ."

"Yes?" I said hopefully.

". . . the end is coming!"

"Thanks," Jon said. "Thanks a lot."

With a whirl of wind and a scatter of ice, the Valkyries rode up into the sky again with their horses.

We looked over the rim to the deep crater below. Steam and fog rolled up from the abyss, so we couldn't see what might be down there. Eerie noises echoed up the rocks. Creaking. Fluttering. The clattering of rocks down the side and onto the frozen surface of the lake.

Jon shook his head. "Oh, man . . ."

"When the volcano erupted a few years ago, a network of ancient mines was uncovered," said Dana. "Scientists haven't explored them all the way. Which is good for us."

It was hard to believe that any of this was good for us.

I held on to the rope and lowered myself onto the steep path that twisted around the inside of the volcano, using my sword as a snow pick to steady myself. Soon we were making the long, winding descent into the crater.

A slow hour later, we stood together on a narrow lip of rock, staring into a ragged black hole in the side of the volcano and wondering.

"The mine entrance?" asked Sydney.

Dana nodded.

"How inviting," Jon added.

Inviting or not, Dana and I stepped inside first, since we had the torches. They didn't help all that much. Darkness closed around the flames so tightly we saw only a few feet ahead. We had to crouch really low to avoid getting our heads sliced off by the jagged rocks hanging from the ceiling. Step-by-step we pressed deeper into the mine, until the way was nearly blocked by huge, stringy cobwebs.

"If a giant spider attacks us," said Jon, "I'm going to be very upset. Of course, I'm starting out pretty upset, so you might not be able to tell the difference. By the way, these mines are abandoned, right?"

Dana burned the cobwebs away and squinted into the darkness. "Probably."

"Probably?" Jon grumbled. "You and the lunch ladies should start a comedy act —"

"Shh. What's that?" said Sydney.

We heard a faint roar from a narrow passage on our left. Cautiously, we stepped in. Soon the roar was all we could hear, echoing all around us. As we walked, the tunnel opened into a cave whose back wall was a rushing waterfall.

"Buried by sound?" said Jon, quoting the riddle. "Do you think the Crystal Rune is behind the waterfall?"

"There's one way to find out." Sydney nudged my arm. "Owen, the lyre."

I was wondering how long it would be before I'd have to use it.

Ever since we had "borrowed" the ancient Lyre of Orpheus from a museum, and since it turned out that I seemed to know how to pluck melodies from its seven strings, we'd relied on the lyre to do some pretty awesome magical stuff. The fact that playing it almost made my brain explode either meant that I really shouldn't be playing it, or that was just some kind of weird price you had to pay to get magic to work for you. Either way, the lyre had saved our lives a few times already, so I endured the pain and sucked it up.

I handed Sydney my torch and took the lyre out of its holster. Holding it close, I plucked first one string, then another. My head instantly began to throb and my eyes felt like fireballs. But the melody was working. In a matter of seconds, the falling water slowed, then thickened like ice, then stopped altogether. It looked like an unmoving curtain with the tunnel continuing beyond it.

"That still impresses me," said Jon. "How does the lyre have any magic left, after all it's been through?"

It *was* impressive. The lyre had been through a lot. I'd used it as a weapon. Its strings had been busted more times than I can remember, but it still made music. I hoped that whatever today would bring, the lyre would remain in one piece.

We quietly approached the frozen curtain, until we heard something in the passage behind us.

Scuffling.

Scratching.

Breathing.

"So," Jon whispered. "The mine isn't abandoned after all."

Sydney held up the torch. In its glow we could see a pack of doglike creatures pad slowly into the cave. There must have been a dozen of them. They had no

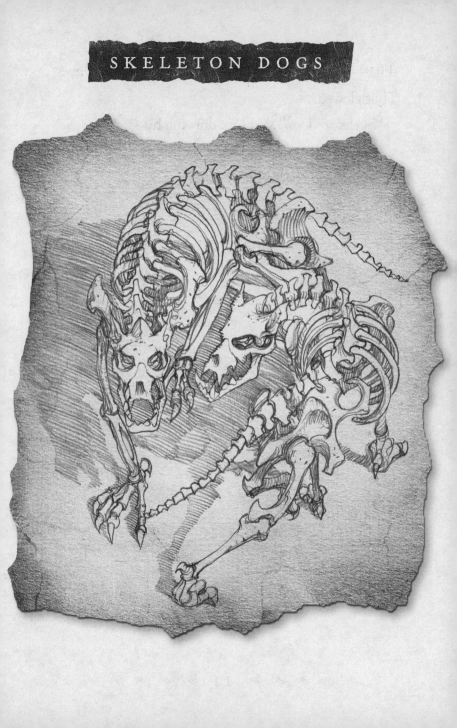

skin — just bones and teeth and skulls and slitty eyes. That glowed.

"Skeleton dogs," said Jon, drawing his sword.

"*Killer* skeleton dogs," Dana said softly.

We had no choice but to run.

CHAPTER TWO

In the Mine! In the Mine!

Sydney and Dana hurled their torches at the dogs. We ducked behind the frozen waterfall as I plucked the lyre's strings in reverse order, releasing the rushing water again.

Eeeeee! shrieked the skeleton dogs. I had a feeling the water wasn't going to stop them.

"Go!" Dana cried. We careened from passage to passage, pursued by the creepy sound of bone feet scraping the floor. Without the torches, we ran in the dark. But the problem with running in the dark is that you hit things. Like each other.

"Ow!" Jon cried.

"Get off me!" Sydney yelled.

"Just follow my voice," Dana called from up ahead.

"It's getting colder," said Jon. "We're going deeper into the mines, farther from the surface. Farther from . . . everything!"

I didn't want to think about it. "This way," I said. I slipped down a side passage and pulled the others with me. It must have tricked the skeleton dogs, because after a while, we couldn't hear their scary feet pawing the stones anymore. As a matter of fact, we couldn't hear anything.

I thumbed the lyre's highest string gently, and a faint golden light shone out. Now we could see that the passage narrowed and ended a few feet ahead. It led nowhere.

"I knew it," Jon groaned. "This is the part where *we're* buried by silence. Behold our crypt. The tomb that time forgot. It was nice knowing you guys.

Though I could do without our slow and agonizing demise —"

"Calm down," said Sydney. "We just have to backtrack."

"And meet those dead dogs again?" said Jon. "No, thanks. I'll wait here."

Sydney glared at him. "Wait for what? To starve to death?"

"Enough!" said Dana. "We'll think of something." She opened her copy of *Bulfinch's Mythology* and started flipping the pages. Finally, she said, "Owen, feel free to inspire us. . . ."

Everyone stared at me. "Oh, sure," I said. "Turn to the kid with the magical lyre."

I plucked one string after the other. I pretended I was working on an idea of how to save us. But I didn't have an idea. I had nothing.

After a few minutes of string-plucking, I frowned to make it look like I was thinking, and walked the whole length of the passage step-by-step, as if I were measuring. I wasn't thinking. I wasn't measuring. I was freaking out.

"Guys," I started.

"What's that?" Jon interrupted me, pointing up to a small round stone inset in the ceiling. It was polished and black — and unlike anything around it.

"Exactly what we're looking for!" I said.

I held up the lyre and, all at once, the reflection of light from the lyre flashed from the stone directly onto the passage floor. It bounced off at an angle, struck the wall near Sydney's head, smacked the floor between Jon's feet, and hit the wall behind Dana, changing color with each new direction. Finally, it came to rest on the wall just over the passage entrance.

The wall burned brightly for a moment in the whole rainbow of colors, then went clear.

And there it was.

A long, slender crystal, set right into the wall.

Dana gasped. "The Crystal Rune of Asgard! We found it!"

The rune was small, a kind of sharp-edged, angular oval, with intersecting lines carved deep inside the crystal. It glowed gently with its own white light.

"Dana, you do the honors," I said.

She stood on her toes and slipped the glassy stone from its niche in the wall. "It's cold. And heavy. My Old Norse is a little rusty, but I think these carvings are a kind of poem. If I can get it right . . ." She frowned, moved her lips silently, and then finally read the lines aloud.

> "Whoever holds this crystal key
> Holds close the fate of Odin's throne."

It was a chilling prophecy. When Dana handed the rune to me, I suddenly understood why Loki was all crazy to get his hands on the thing. There was something powerful and electric running through the stone. But the fact that the poem actually foretold the end of the Norse world, the Twilight of the Gods, was why Loki wanted the rune more than anything in the world.

"Loki knows that the only way for him to survive the Twilight of the Gods is in Odin's throne," I said. "With this rune, he can have that. That's why he wants it so much."

"But we have it now," said Sydney. "And I think we need to get this straight to Odin before anything else —"

Thud-d-d. Thud-d-d. Footsteps echoed down the passage and into the cave.

My senses buzzed. "Dogs?" I whispered. I holstered the lyre and drew my sword along with the others. There was silence for a moment. Then came a weird, inhuman shriek. And the rustle of . . . hooves.

"Sounds like something bigger than dogs," whispered Jon. "I knew this was where we'd end our days —"

"Leave the children be, you nasty goblins!" boomed a voice. "Take that! And that!"

A flash of metal and the howl of voices filled the air.

"This way, children!" shouted the booming voice. Suddenly, there was a man standing at the mouth of the passage. In one hand he held a broadsword; in the other, a torch sizzling with red flames. He was huge, with long blond hair, a big beard, and a smile.

"You'd better come with me," the man said when we didn't budge. "These rock goblins are hungry!"

A small army of green-skinned creatures swarmed out from the rocks. They were as skinny as stick figures, with tight green skin, curving talons, and hoofed feet. I resisted the sudden urge to throw up.

The man swung his blade sharply, and two goblins jumped away screaming. The pack started pelting him with rocks and daggers, but nearly everything bounced off the man's arms and legs as if he were made of iron.

"Oh, come on!" he crowed. "Is that all you have?" He jiggled the daggers out of his arms and tossed them back, then swung his massive sword in a wide circle to clear a path. "You kids can scurry out any time you want, you know!" he said.

We scurried.

While the man hacked a path through the goblins, we tore through the mines, Dana clutching the rune close to her. As we burst out of the tunnels and clambered back up the path to the surface, the man tossed his torch into the cave and the goblins retreated. That was when we finally saw the full size of our rescuer. He was a man at least seven feet tall, with massive muscles and bulging arms, covered with furs from his

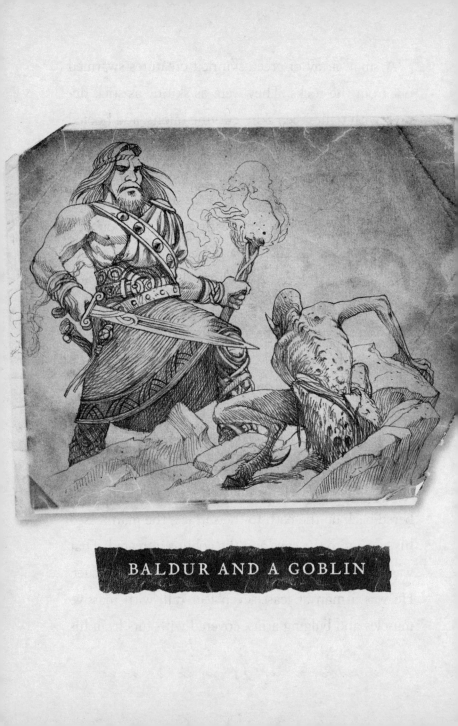

BALDUR AND A GOBLIN

shoulders to his chunky boots. We could see long, flowing blond hair when he removed a helmet the size of a fire hydrant, with a white horn curving up from the center.

"Are you . . . Odin?" I mumbled, huffing for breath.

The man cracked a smile. "Me? *Pffft!* I wish. I'm Baldur, Odin's son. Well, one of his sons. He has a few." With little effort he rolled a giant stone over the mine entrance. "That should hold those nasty goblins for a while," he said. "They had rune necklaces, did you see? Loki must be nearby." Then he paused. "Hold on —"

He twisted his elbow around. There were three goblin daggers sticking out of it.

"I thought I had an itch!" Baldur said with a growly laugh, tugging the daggers out and snapping them between his fingers like toothpicks. Then he turned back to us and grinned. "I see you have the Lyre of Orpheus. There's good magic in that thing — though not as much as in that rune you have."

"We weren't stealing it," said Dana quickly.

"I know," said Baldur. "I recognize Sindr's handiwork on your armor, so I know you must be friends."

"But the goblins stabbed you," said Jon. I swear he hadn't blinked in two minutes. "Are you indestructible or something?"

Baldur smiled. "Well, I'm a god, of course. But my father, Odin, also added an extra charm to make me invincible —"

Sydney gasped. "I know why! It's because of your bad dreams, isn't it?"

The Norse god blinked. "Yes. I've been having dreams where I . . . die. But how could you possibly know that?"

Dana pulled out her copy of *Bulfinch's Mythology*. "It's in my book. We've all been reading it. There's a story about you and your dreams."

Baldur frowned, but before he could say anything more, the squeal of goblins echoed and the rock over the mine entrance shifted a little. Baldur narrowed his eyes at the rock. "Take the rune to my father. He's in Asgard, at the top of that glacier."

He blew out a long breath, and the clouds cleared enough for us to see a giant glacier slanting up beyond the volcano toward a mountain range nearby. The uppermost tip of the glacier was lost in fog.

"Asgard lies at the very top," he said. "Follow the glacier up. And keep that rune from prying eyes. Now excuse me, I've got to make sure these goblins don't follow you. Hurry to Asgard!"

Baldur leaped back to the mouth of the cave, swinging his broadsword at the escaping goblins.

"You heard what Baldur said," said Dana, quickly coiling the rope over her shoulder. "To Asgard!"

CHAPTER THREE

FROM HUT TO HALL

THE GLACIER WAS A VAST FIELD OF ICE, SLOPING UP from the northern rim of the volcano to somewhere completely shrouded by clouds. It looked like a straight shot, but the thing about glaciers is that they're slippery — so climbing them isn't easy. Two wobbly steps forward, one back. It took forever to make any progress.

Plus, it was getting colder by the second, our armor was freezing, and we had to keep breaking icicles off our helmets. All I wanted — all I *really* wanted — was to lie down and sleep.

On top of that, it began to snow. Hard.

"We're going to get so lost," Jon said. "I can't even see my own hands."

Dana passed the rune to Sydney and uncoiled the rope from her shoulder. "Let's use the rope to tie ourselves to one another."

"That way if one of us falls, we all fall?" said Jon.

Sydney slipped the rune inside her armor and gave Jon a look. "No. This way, we don't lose *you*."

We looped the rope around our waists, and just in time, too. When a blast of wind cleared the whirling snow for a second, Jon was tiptoeing inches from the edge of a deep chasm.

"Ack!" cried Jon. "We almost lost me!"

I looked down into the chasm, but couldn't see the bottom. I kicked a slab of ice off the edge. It dropped fast, exploding into pieces with each ledge it struck on the way down.

"Ohhh . . ."

I turned to the others. "Who said that?"

"Ohhh . . ."

"Someone's out there," Sydney said, pointing into the spinning snow. "Hello?"

"Ohhh . . . help!"

We made our way forward, following the sound. Soon we saw an old woman dressed in rags. Her hands were stretched out in front of her, searching the air as if to find her way.

"Wait, is this a mirage?" Jon said, shrinking back.

"If it's not, then what is an old lady doing out here?" Dana whispered. "Ma'am? Stop —"

"I need to find my dog. He fell into the ravine. There he is!" the woman cried, stepping to the edge and pointing to a small dog limping back and forth on a ledge some ten feet below. "I have to save my poor puppy!"

"No!" said Dana. "I'll get your dog for you. You stay here. Guys, give me some slack."

"What?" I said. There was no way. But Dana gave me a look that told me she'd made up her mind. She was going. Keeping the rope tight around her waist, Dana edged down the chasm wall while we lowered her foot by foot onto the ledge. The dog backed away from her, but she motioned it over and stroked its head. "It's all right. It's okay, Mr. Puppy. Let's climb back up. Here we go. . . ."

"Dana, be careful," Jon said.

Dana held the dog close, and we pulled her gently to the top of the chasm.

"My hero!" the woman cried, as the dog leaped into her arms. "Now all of you must come with me. My hut is nearby, so you can warm yourselves. Follow me!"

Laughing, the woman clutched Dana's wrist as if it were a lifeline, unhooked her rope, and pulled her into the whirling snowstorm.

"We need to keep moving," said Sydney. "We can't stay."

"Only long enough to warm up," said Jon.

"Dana?" I called. She didn't answer. "Dana! Wait for us!"

We lost sight of her for a second, and I didn't like it. The snow was whipping around like a tornado, and it was all I could do not to be swept into the chasm myself. We plowed ahead for what seemed like ten

OWEN

SYDNEY   JON

DANA   OLD WOMAN

DOG

RAVINE

GLACIER

THE RAVINE

minutes (but was probably only a few seconds), until we finally saw the woman's home. It was a tiny hut wedged under a ridge of glacier. The wind blew like a hurricane across the ice, and it struck me that the hut hardly seemed strong enough to survive a good rain, never mind an Icelandic winter.

"Dana?" I said. "Dana? Where are you —"

And there she was, already squeezing out the little hut door, her arms full of bundles.

"The nice lady gave us food!" She held up a loaf of bread and a bunch of grapes.

Jon leaped on them. "I'm so hungry!"

"And she gave me a special flower because I was so heroic," said Dana, showing off a sprig of green with white berries tucked into her helmet. "Mistletoe. Cool, huh?"

"Christmas mistletoe? Where did she find that?" Sydney asked. "We're on a glacier. Nothing grows here."

Dana shrugged. "Well, I like it."

The whole episode was weird, but then again, what *wasn't* weird about the last few days? I went to the hut and peeked in the door. The old woman sat on her bed in the corner, the puppy at her feet. "Thank you," I said. "We have to go now."

Dana whispered over my shoulder. "She told me we just keep going up."

"My favorite direction," Jon grumbled.

But we had a job to do — we had to find Dana's parents and stop Loki. So we walked on.

And on and on.

We huddled together and pushed through the snow. Whenever we found ourselves trekking on level ground, we knew we were off course, so we searched until we found a slope and traveled up again. Another hour passed before we burst through the storm and came out above the clouds. The snowstorm swirled beneath us.

Then Sydney jumped. "Ow!" She yanked the Crystal Rune from her armor. It was beaming like a laser.

Dana gasped. "Just like in the legends!"

The rune was probably the most beautiful thing any of us had ever seen. Now its light suddenly arced across the glacier to a point in the near distance, where it stopped cold.

"Well, that's weird," said Sydney. "Light doesn't actually work like that — it usually fades out. But then again, this is a magic rune, so anything's possible."

When we approached the glowing point of light, it began to change color. At first, it shimmered silver. Then blue. Then crimson. Finally, the spot beamed with a white light more brilliant than the ice itself. And the more we watched, the more the light grew up from the ground and took shape in the air.

"It's forming a door!" I said.

As we stepped up to the door, it opened wide.

"Asgard," Dana said softly.

We passed through the door. It closed behind us, and I had the sudden feeling of not caring if I were trapped inside that door forever.

Where nothing but ice had existed only seconds before, now we could see a city of snow and stone, of crystal and silver. Tall buildings made of blue and white granite, gleaming with the sheen of moonlight, rose from hills of snow and green valleys as far as the eye could see. It was so deeply beautiful, so calm, that for the first time in weeks I felt at peace.

"Stop where you stand!" boomed a deep voice.

I took a look at the guy who had spoken and I nearly choked. I was getting the idea that the standard Norse god was a cross between a bodybuilder and a model. The guy who marched up to us had bigger and bushier blond hair than Baldur's, was about a foot taller, and wielded a bunch of fairly unimaginable weapons — like a seven-bladed spear, a pair of winged arrows hovering in the air, something that resembled a Frisbee made of flaming thorns, and a long pole with a big golden claw on the end of it.

Then we saw a huge rainbow-colored bridge rising up behind him.

"Are you . . . Odin?" asked Jon.

"Ha!" the man boomed. "I am a toddler compared to the great Odin! I am the Watch guard of the bridge to Asgard. And I know you. You are Owen, Jon, Sydney, and Dana."

"We have to see Odin," I said. "We have . . . this . . ." Sydney held out the Crystal Rune.

All at once, the ground shook with the sound of a herd of horses galloping over the bridge.

Only it wasn't a herd.

It was a single horse.

With eight legs.

A god in a horned helmet rode tall in the horse's saddle. His hair was so blond, it was almost white. By the massive hammer slung over his shoulder, we knew who he was.

"Thor!" Jon cried. "Whoa, there are whole movies about you!"

Thor slapped the reins of the eight-legged horse until he practically rode over us. Halting abruptly, he said, "Odin the magnificent, my father, requests you at the weapons forge! Mount his magical horse and come!"

It's not the kind of request you think twice about.

So we mounted our second magical horse of the day.

CHAPTER FOUR

BALDUR'S GAME

WE CLUNG TO ONE ANOTHER FOR DEAR LIFE AS THE giant eight-legged horse galloped down into the green valley, through a forest of tall pine trees, and up to the high hills, eating up the miles in minutes.

It was hard to breathe, but it wasn't long before we saw Valhalla, the giant hall at the northernmost point of Asgard.

Valhalla was a hall the size of a small city. It was made of wood and stone, covered with ice, and beaming with silver light. Its high walls were jammed with warriors. But the amazing horse bounded on until we came to a place where furnaces and forges were pumping black smoke from tall chimneys. We recognized the Valkyries' horses tethered outside.

"This is the forge Baldur told us about," said Sydney as we dismounted. "Kind of like how the Cyclopes used the power plant in Pinewood Bluffs as their forge."

"My father, Odin, is preparing for war," said Thor.

We passed heaps of breastplates, stacks of helmets, swords of all widths and lengths. Spears and axes leaned against the high walls of the forge. Some that lay cooling on the ground had melted the snow down to the brown earth.

Miss Hilda poked her head out of the forge. "He's expecting you!" I couldn't help feeling relieved to see her familiar face.

We entered, and immediately felt the heat of the ovens. The ceiling was charred black as smoke poured out a chimney at the top. More weapons gleamed inside, some sooty and black, some white-hot. But all

VALHALLA

this was nothing compared to the god standing in front of us.

Odin — this time it *had* to be him — towered over a giant anvil, running his hand up and down the flat edges of a three-bladed sword, each blade as long as a ski and twice as wide. He turned the weapon in the firelight, weighing it, then making swift curlicues in the air.

Flames from the nearest furnace beamed on the god's golden face, except where a black eye patch covered his left eye. Thor joined the three Valkyries and stood behind Odin.

"Is it good, my lord?" said a small, lumpy man half the size of Odin. His eyes looked expectantly from the sword to the god.

"It will serve, Sindr," Odin said. "It will serve well, indeed."

Odin turned toward us, the sword smoking, almost like it was breathing. "Welcome, children. My daughters" — he waved his hand at the lunch ladies — "alerted me to your coming. You find Asgard on the eve of war."

We bowed.

"Asgard is beautiful," said Sydney. "So is Valhalla."

"Only as long as we protect them," Odin said gravely. "And only for now. Let's hope our home doesn't fall into the depths, as Loki wishes. Come. Look."

We followed Odin out of the forge, to a rise overlooking a vast sea. "Since I learned the mystery of the runes, for which I sacrificed my eye, I have known of Loki's eventual betrayal. It is written that he shall come over the Sea of Asgard in ships made from dead men's fingernails." He peered out over the water. "Make no mistake, Loki is a god, and powerful. But his power comes from trickery and evil, not from good. Therein is our one chance to stop him."

"We found the Crystal Rune," said Jon. "Show him, Syd."

Sydney removed it from her armor and held it out.

The rune's white light flickered brightly, but Odin's face grew dark. He took the rune from Sydney, looked it over, then passed it to me.

"I wish it had never been found, never been created," he said. "The Crystal Rune of Asgard is a key to

Valhalla's deepest secret. . . ." He paused, saw the holster on my back. "You carry a weapon?"

"A lyre," I said. "It belonged to Orpheus."

Odin nodded grimly. "Magic older than even the Crystal Rune. Amid all these weapons, you may have use of your lyre here."

"What is the rune's secret?" asked Dana, half turned away, her eyes fixed on the sea below us. "It would probably help us to know."

Odin shook his head. "The time for explanations will come soon enough. For now, not even Loki knows its power — not that that will stop him." Odin breathed out, then nodded toward Dana, who had stepped away and was staring out over the crest of the hill to the sea below. "Your friend seems . . . deep in thought."

"Loki's Draugs took her parents to Niflheim," I said. "They knew too much about the Crystal Rune."

"And that is why I keep its secret close," Odin said.

Just then, Baldur raced up the hill to the crest and embraced his father, brother, and sisters. A handful of other super-blond heroes called Baldur over, laughing, and began testing their weapons — first against one another, then on Baldur himself.

"Strike as you may!" He laughed. "I am invincible, charmed against every harm!"

"Not *every* harm," said Dana quietly.

"Father, look," Thor called. "Your ravens have returned."

The black and white ravens we'd seen before swooped out of the sky. One sat on each of Odin's ridiculously broad shoulders. "What say you?" he asked the birds. "Speak so all may understand."

"Ships gather in the eastern ocean," squawked the black raven. At this point, nothing should have surprised me, but I couldn't help thinking how cool it was that I understood the ravens.

"Loki's flagship leads them, though he is not with them," said the white raven.

Before we could puzzle out what that meant, a flare went up on the plain below and an armada of black-hulled ships appeared on the horizon. Odin's expression grew even more grim. "Marshal the armies. Heroes, take up arms to meet our enemy!"

Everyone started after the great god, but when I turned to Dana, she was staring at Baldur. She didn't move, except to slide the mistletoe from her helmet.

"Dana?" I said. "Are you all right?"

Odin turned and fixed his eyes on her. "Is that . . . no . . ." His eyes flashed from Baldur to Dana. "Not you — not here —"

"What's going on?" said Jon.

Dana lifted her arm high over her head and threw the sprig of mistletoe at Baldur.

Every other weapon had bounced off him harmlessly, but for some reason the mistletoe struck Baldur deeply in the neck. He cried out and fell to his knees. With a sigh as loud as the wind, he slid to the ground, eyes blank, body still.

"My son!" boomed Odin. "The traitor has killed my son!"

"Traitor?" I said. There had to be some mistake. "Dana?"

"Brother!" shouted Thor.

I pulled Dana toward me. "What did you —"

Only it wasn't Dana anymore.

Her familiar features twisted and shrank in an instant, and she was suddenly the old woman. Then she was a dwarf, then a child, then a bear, then a snake-headed old man. I couldn't believe what I was seeing. Jon and Sydney gaped, mouths hanging open. Finally, we were staring at Loki himself, his silver armor beaming in the flames of the furnace.

"Loki, you fiend!" Odin cried.

"You forget that I am a shape-shifter! And this was *so* simple!" Loki hissed. "I knew that the lowly mistletoe was passed over by Odin's charm. I needled the secret out of the Sybil. Thank you, children, for allowing me to switch with your friend. For bringing me here, into Asgard! With Baldur's death, all is fulfilled. Ragnarok begins now!"

"What have you done with Dana?" I cried, drawing my sword.

"Why, she's joined her parents in Niflheim, of course!" he sneered. "But don't worry your little heads about her. I'll see to her personally . . . when I rule all the worlds!" With a swift flash of his armored hand, he tore the Crystal Rune from me, slicing my palm open. "Now the rune is mine!"

Enraged, Thor threw his hammer at Loki, but Loki became a deer and leaped out of the way. Then his hooves stretched into talons. Clutching the Crystal Rune to his chest, he became a bird and flew straight up and out over the cold sea to join his approaching ships.

"Baldur!" Odin wailed at the top of his lungs, and Valhalla trembled on its foundations. "Children," he shouted, "the reign of the gods is coming to its terrible end. We postpone Baldur's journey to the land of the dead. First we fight, then we mourn our lost son." He raised an arm in the air. "All heroes — to the shore!"

CHAPTER FIVE

WRITTEN IN THE BEGINNING

WE WATCHED, STUNNED, AS FOUR GODS TOOK UP Baldur's limp body and walked slowly up the hill to Valhalla.

"I've known forever that Loki is evil," Sydney said, wiping tears from her cheeks. "We all have. But this — killing Odin's son right in front of us — this is different. This is . . . worse."

"What just happened?" Jon said. "Where's Dana?"

I wiped the blood from the shallow cut on my hand. "Loki must have switched places with Dana in the hut. We lost sight of them for what, a minute? Long enough. Loki probably changed Fenrir into the dog. And now Dana's . . . in the Underworld!"

"We need every sword!" Thor shouted. He turned to us. "Children, are you with us?"

Jon looked at me. "We have to save Dana, don't we?"

Sydney's face was as hard as a stone. "That's the most important thing."

My mind was spinning. "But as long as Loki's up here, he won't be in Niflheim. Dana and her parents are safe," I said. "And if we can defeat him —"

All at once, we heard a long, queasy note that sounded like it was played on the bone of some long-dead animal.

"Who comes now?" Odin boomed.

"It is I, Kingu, with my army!" called a voice nearly as loud in reply.

We turned, and our friend from the Babylonian Underworld — a god clad in scorpion armor —

marched before an army of lion-headed warriors. Next to him trod his son, the massive stone giant, Ullikummi.

"Children, we traveled through your world to join this war," Kingu said, approaching us.

"As did I, the god of the Egyptian Underworld,

Anubis," said a jackal-headed creature at least eight feet tall from boots to ears, who marched in behind us. "My canine warriors are at your service, Odin!"

"And look!" said Sydney. "Our old friend!"

Over a distant hill strode an enormous red-armored god. It was Hades himself, king of the Greek

Underworld. With him marched the great heroes, Odysseus, Hercules, Jason, and a thousand others.

My head swam. We were witnessing a massive gathering of gods and heroes, and it was awesome. Also, terrifying. Ragnarok — the Twilight of the Gods — was going to be huge.

The three Underworld leaders joined us on a plain high above the sea, while their armies massed at the shore below. Odin greeted and embraced Hades, Anubis, and Kingu in turn. It was a very strange sight.

"It was Hades who showed us the way through your village, children," said Anubis.

"How is it . . ." I started, but couldn't go on.

"It burns still," said Kingu softly, "but without Loki, the fire monsters fell under my command once more. They are back below, where they belong."

"Odin, your allies unite to stop Loki's invasion because of these children here," boomed Hades. He looked right at me with his fiery eyes. It was hard to hold his gaze. "These children alone assured our allegiance."

Odin breathed deeply and turned to us, too. "I shall help you find your friend. If we survive this day."

The black and white ravens circled over Odin's head, chattering. He answered with a swift nod, then peered out across the waves. "Loki's ships will land soon. Kingu, Hades, line your armies along the shore to the east. Anubis, to the west. Create a corridor across the plains to the bridge. In his greed for my throne, Loki cannot help but enter. We shall trap him at the bridge!"

No sooner had the Underworld gods moved their armies to the shore, than we heard the faint pounding of drums. Soon, the drums were all we could hear, battering out a rhythm for the oarsmen on Loki's warships. Rowing the lead ship were giants covered in ice, with long white hair to their shoulders, dented armor, furs, and enormous boots. There were a dozen of them, and they were taller than oak trees.

This didn't bode well.

Sydney gasped softly. "Those must be the Frost Giants," she said. "I remember them from Dana's book."

Then . . . suddenly . . . silence.

No sound but the lapping of waves. The whole world seemed to wait, holding its breath.

I looked at Jon. "This is it —"

THOOM!

THOOM!

The ground shook. Even before the first ships landed on the far side of the bridge, the enormous stony-faced Frost Giants, led by Loki himself, climbed down into the water and charged toward solid ground, bypassing the bridge entirely. The earth shook beneath our feet as the giants thudded up onto the land.

"Heroes! To the shore!" Odin shouted. Wave upon wave of armored men and gods charged down the fields to meet the approaching ships. At the same time, the Frost Giants thundered up from the shore, heaving boulders at the Norsemen.

Loki leaped ahead of the giants, swinging his silver sword, booming out commands. Meanwhile, his army of beasts — angry, evil, and fearless — charged off the boats onto the Asgard bridge.

Jon turned to Odin. "What can we do to help?"

Odin stood with Thor but seemed alone, the wind brushing his hair and beard. The golden glow of his face was now a somber gray. "Now that I see the size of Loki's great force, my heart quakes in sorrow. The end of the gods may happen today. You *can* help. . . ."

Odin needed something from *us*? Three kids who were way out of our element?

He lowered his head to us. "Children, enter the high throne room. Destroy my throne. Make certain no piece of it stands."

"But, Father, why?" asked Thor. "That throne has been the seat of your power since the beginning of time. It is indestructible!"

Odin breathed in a long breath, his eyes scanning the roiling battlefield below. "Thor, my son, not even you know this. Only I know the reason the throne must be destroyed. Only I know its terrible truth. It must now be told."

My mind reeled. I was terrified of what he might say. What secret could make the chief Norse god confide in humans? In kids?

"The Crystal Rune," Odin said, "is nothing less than an ancient key. That is why I tried to keep it hidden. It transforms my throne into a cursed engine, a device of destruction so vile you could never imagine.

Its single purpose is to grind all the worlds to dust. It is a Doomsday machine, fashioned at the moment that Asgard came to be. It is the curse beneath the beauty. It is the end written in the beginning. That is why I have protected it for eons."

He looked up at the high towers of Valhalla. "I built this great hall with my own hands for one reason: to keep — no, to imprison — the terror within."

"Father," said Thor, glancing at the battlefield below, then back to Odin, "you lived like this? For centuries?"

Odin placed his armored hand on Thor's shoulder. "From the beginning. Children, you know the inscription on the rune?"

I recited it from memory.

"Whoever holds this crystal key
Holds close the fate of Odin's throne."

Odin nodded. "Turn the rune upside down, and you will see its other inscription, the words that complete the poem." He spoke them.

"Come Ragnarok, when all is gone,
Great Odin's throne alone shall be."

Loki yelled somewhere below. "Draug archers — take the field!" The battle was ramping up, and all we could do was stare at Odin in shock.

"But what you're saying isn't in any of the Norse myths, is it?" asked Sydney. "Dana would have mentioned it."

Arrows rose like a black cloud of crows.

"It is a story for the end times only," Odin said, watching the arrows fall. "Not knowing the Crystal Rune's true power, Loki believes that it will claim my throne for him. He will use it and let loose its terrifying, grim secret. You must destroy the throne before this can happen."

"But if it's indestructible, how?" Jon said.

"Baldur was invincible except for the sting of the lowly mistletoe," said Odin. "There is always a way. Perhaps with magic older than the rune itself." He looked at my holster.

"The lyre?" I said. "But it's so banged up."

"Owen Brown, use your lyre," Odin said. "Find the single note that will turn my throne to ash, that will destroy what is indestructible."

No pressure or anything. Just a command to save the world, given by a Norse god. No big deal.

I remembered how we struggled in the Babylonian Underworld until I discovered that each object and place resonated with its own frequency. Would that knowledge help us here?

I ran my fingers along the arms of the lyre, thinking about how beautiful it had been in the museum when we first saw it. It had been through, well, a couple of Underworlds since then. And now that Dana was trapped in Niflheim, the thing I'd always feared might actually happen: I could lose her forever. We would need the lyre to rescue her, too — but I didn't know if it could hold up until then.

"If you cannot destroy my throne before Loki arrives," Odin said, "not just Asgard, but all the worlds — yours included — shall fall."

"But isn't it written that destroying your throne will also . . . destroy you?" asked Thor in alarm.

Odin nodded. "A small price to pay for the survival of the worlds. Now, lead the children to Valhalla. Help them as you can —"

Arrows continued crashing onto the field. Kingu's lion-headed troops scattered. Ullikummi swatted the arrows away, but still more fell. The battlefield crawled with shapes, as if the solid ground were boiling. Monsters from Niflheim. Beasts of every description. Dead men. Millions of Draugs, Frost Giants, Hill Giants, Mountain Giants.

All to put Loki on Odin's throne.

"Go!" said Odin. "Prevent the end, if you can!"

Leaving the field in a daze, stunned by what we'd been asked to do, we climbed the final hill to the great hall of Valhalla. From its front gate, what we saw was a horrifying sight. A caravan of catapults rolled off Loki's ships and plowed across the bridge onto land, firing as they advanced. The sky was black with arrows and projectiles. Explosions of liquid fire set the fields aflame. Great snow-headed elephants stormed off the ships at a gallop, trumpeting wildly as they scattered Anubis and his Egyptian forces.

"Inside, quickly," said Thor.

Once inside the outermost walls of Valhalla, we mounted one stairway after another, steep and tall and almost vertical, to a level above the walls. There were more stairs to climb, and more, and more. I turned to look at what was going on below.

Hades waded into a herd of spiked beasts, blades swinging, his spiky red armor dented but not breached. The bellowing roars of the beasts rang among Valhalla's heights.

Thor pulled me away. "We are nearly there. Hurry!"

We climbed steps and entered the great hall. It was an open room made of stone. Wooden rafters criss-crossed the ceiling, which rose to a height I could barely see. Benches lined the hall from end to end.

"This is where the Norse gods feasted," said Thor. "Until today."

He led us from the banquet hall and up more high steps until we came to a flat terrace in the open air, where Baldur's body lay on a platform, waiting for his final voyage to the Underworld. Behind Baldur stood a tall arch of blue stone. Beyond it, we could see only darkness.

"Go through the arch," Thor said, "then travel to the end of the ramparts. The throne stands at the very top of Valhalla. I cannot pass this point."

"Why not?" asked Sydney.

Thor pointed to words carved over the arch. "It translates to 'No god nor man can enter here but the All-High Odin Himself.'"

"So Loki can't go in, either," said Jon.

"Loki is a shape-shifter," said Sydney. "He'll find a way."

"But we can go in," I said, suddenly understanding. "Because we're not gods or men. We're . . . kids."

There came a growl so loud and deep that the stones quaked beneath our feet.

"What is *that?*" asked Sydney.

"One of the many signs that foretell our doom!" said Thor.

Comforting.

We ran to the edge of the terrace and looked at the

field below. Fenrir, the red wolf and son of Loki, was now as large as a house. When he opened his jaws, they seemed to reach from the ground to the clouds. An inferno of flame burst out between his fangs, scorching large swaths of the green fields.

"I cannot stay!" Thor said, stepping away from us. "I would tell you, 'May the gods be with you,' but I fear you're on your own. Good luck. It's all we have now!"

And without another word, Thor raced in great strides down from Valhalla and the mountain, leaping over rocks and stumps. He jumped from ledge to ledge, back to the field where Fenrir leaped, fiery-mouthed, at Odin himself.

CHAPTER SIX

THE ICE DRAGON

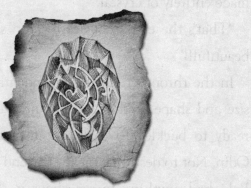

JON, SYDNEY, AND I STARED DOWN AT THE FIELD FROM the doorway of the great hall, and suddenly it hit me that we *were* on our own. I couldn't tell what I felt. Would Asgard really fall today? Would Loki rule? Would our worlds crumble?

I looked at the lyre in my hands. It seemed so old and frail.

"Come on," said Jon. "Odin may not survive, but let's do what we have to do."

We slipped under the arch and started running up stairways to the summit and Odin's throne. Finally, we came to a place open to the sky, a high, flat terrace of white stone polished to a glassy sheen. At the far end stood a tall throne, as high and wide as a house, made entirely of crystal.

"That's the engine of death?" Jon said. "It's so . . . beautiful!"

In the throne's back was an indentation the exact size and shape of the Crystal Rune. I felt my knees ready to buckle. To destroy it meant the death of Odin. Not to destroy it meant the end of our world, if Loki had anything to say about it. "This lyre isn't going to do anything at all —"

Then we heard something weird. It sounded like crunching and cracking and stomping, but it wasn't coming from the noisy battlefield. It was coming from the forest just below Valhalla's uppermost level — just below us.

"Oh, please," said Jon. "Tell me it's not him."

Sydney ran to the edge of the wall and looked down. "It's him."

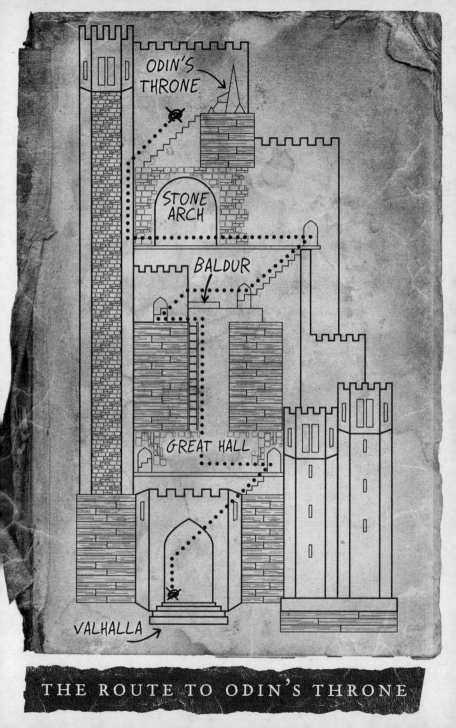

ODIN'S THRONE

STONE ARCH

BALDUR

GREAT HALL

VALHALLA

THE ROUTE TO ODIN'S THRONE

And it was.

While his armies blasted the fields below, Loki had somehow gotten away and was now making his way up the north side of the mountain. In one of his armored hands, he grasped the Crystal Rune he had stolen from us. On either side of him were Frost Giants, uprooting trees as they came. Behind them, a beast that looked vaguely like an oversize ox, with a forehead of iron horns, was dragging a giant battering ram.

My heart pounded like a drum. "How did he get away from the battle?"

"He's a shape-shifter, remember?" said Sydney. "Odin needs to know he's here."

But when we looked down, we saw Fenrir twist his giant head and blast a huge fireball across the field directly at Odin.

Thor leaped for his father, throwing him out of the way as the ground exploded in flame.

"Odin is busy. So are the others," said Jon, scanning the field. "Maybe Kingu —"

WHOOM!

The walls of Valhalla rang like a bell and burst open with a blast.

"Valhalla is breached!" I cried, whipping out the lyre. "We have to destroy the throne!"

In what seemed like a matter of moments, we heard crashing stones and shattering timbers. The walls echoed with the sound of Loki bellowing. And suddenly, he was blasting his way through stones and ice and wooden beams, past Baldur's body, up the last set of stairs until he stood outside the final arch to the throne, the arch that Thor couldn't enter.

Loki's dark eyes smirked as he read the inscription on the crown of the arch. The horns on his head twisted and coiled through the woven bands of his terrifying helmet.

I drew in a breath and slowly plucked a string, knowing it might mean the end of Odin. *Plang-g-g.* It echoed against the stones, then faded. It wasn't the right note. I set my fingers on the next string.

"He's doing it again," said Sydney, pulling me back with her.

"How many ways can one guy be ugly?" Jon muttered.

Quite a few, it turned out. First, he was a clawed beast with six legs, then a serpent, then a woolly creature with fiery horns, then a wormlike man with no bones, and a skeleton with no skin. Then, finally, standing among the broken walls of Valhalla, was a dragon.

A dragon made of ice.

His silver armor had become a scaly hide, making him look like a crazy machine — a cross between a robot and a reptile, a prehistoric serpent, a beast made of spikes and jagged scales. His head was enormous, and the gleaming Crystal Rune swung on a silver chain around his neck.

Lifting a clawed foot high, he stepped under the arch and onto the ramparts leading to the throne.

"We have to stop him here," Sydney said. "Jon, your sword —"

Both swords flashed out as my friends stood side by side, ready to guard me.

My breath seemed to have stopped. I could barely

move my fingers. This was really happening. I plucked the lyre's second string. It sang across the air and faded.

Loki roared, a horrible sound that made my insides twist. His horns, normally clawing like creepy fingers, had frozen as sharp as blades. His wings crackled as they stretched from one wall to the other, a full fifty feet or more. I looked down at the little lyre in my hands. It seemed like such a lame weapon now.

"I claim my throne," Loki said in a weird, slithery voice as he strode forward. "But please don't stand aside. Try to prevent me. I shall enjoy the sport of destroying you. And it will be such fun to tell Dana Runson of your last minutes —"

Before we knew what was happening, Loki lunged at Jon, then swung a claw and tore the lyre from my hands. It flew through the air, struck the icy floor, and crashed into the base of the throne. It must have sent a pain rocketing into my head, because I blurted out the dumbest thing possible before I could stop myself.

"Give up," I said.

Loki laughed. "Are you speaking to me?" he said. "Or to your little friends?"

With a flick of his tail, he slammed the base of the arch behind him. Strangely, it was suddenly as if we were inside an actual room, rather than being beneath the sky. The sharp noises from the battlefield were muffled and distant.

"Now we are alone," Loki said, slowly clawing his way forward. "Every step of the way, you have been there, slowing my progress, clouding my dream."

"It was pretty cloudy to begin with," Sydney said.

Loki sneered at her. "Hades. Kingu. Anubis. You've turned them all against me. You . . . *children*! The amusing part is that it only makes my work easier. For now I can defeat all my enemies in a single battle, a battle that ends with my taking Odin's throne as my own. And, thanks to you, I have the key."

"No one but Odin can sit in Odin's throne," I said.

"Except the possessor of the rune," Loki said, holding it up. "I can read, you know — 'Whoever holds this crystal key holds close the fate of Odin's throne.'"

"Except there's more," I said. " 'Come Ragnarok, when all is gone, great Odin's throne alone shall be.' That means not even you, Loki. That means nothing at all will survive . . . except the throne itself."

I felt if we could just keep Loki busy long enough, Odin would get there. Or Thor. Or Hades. But the distant battle seemed farther away than ever, and the lyre was now thirty feet away from me, possibly busted, a worthless mess of wood and wire.

But if we didn't have the lyre, we didn't have much. So I had to try to get it, however I could.

Loki slid one clawed foot forward. In three moves, he could be at the base of the throne. In two more, he could insert the rune into the throne. This was it.

I glanced at my friends. Sydney was on one side of the room, Jon was in the middle, and I was on the other side. While Loki edged along the wall nearest the courtyard below, I saw my chance.

Just a little more . . .

Come on . . .

"Charge him!" I cried.

CHAPTER SEVEN

THE RUNE
AND THE THRONE

"Wait, what?" said Sydney.

"*Charge* him?" said Jon.

I was the only one who moved. But maybe that worked for me. As Loki's dragon head swung around to look at each of us, I raced at him, then faked a lunge with my sword, spun, ducked, and hacked down as hard as I could. The blow on his left front leg rang in my hands as if I had tried to break open a stone. But the thrust was powerful enough to send a shiver through his body. I heard a crackle of ice and pressed all my weight on the sword.

Sydney and Jon were suddenly with me, thrusting their swords into the same leg. Loki shook himself free and began to slide down the stairs, howling and clutching wildly at us. Sydney tried to pull us back from the edge of the stairs. She would have done it, too, except for the long reach of Loki's tail. He swept all three of us off the ground and we fell with him — thirty feet to the courtyard below, barely missing Baldur's body. The stones cracked beneath the dragon's weight. Jon, Sydney, and I thudded on the floor, hard.

I don't know if we passed out or what, but by the time I opened my eyes, Loki was hobbling back toward the stairs, dragging his wounded leg.

"Jon! Syd!" I called. "We clipped his leg. We can stop him!"

"Just us?" said Jon, groaning for breath. "Have you *looked* at us lately, Owen? We're . . . nothing! We're just kids!"

"That got us this far," Sydney said. "Come *on*!"

Despite his wounded leg and a cracked wing he must have gotten in the fall, Loki dragged himself up the stairs to the level of the throne. We scrambled after him. When we reached the ramparts, Sydney cried, "Owen, watch out!"

Too late. Loki snapped his tail like a whip and swept me across the floor. Jon jumped over the moving tail, then plunged his sword into Loki's cracked wing. The dragon screeched and flung his wing forward, sending both Jon and Sydney tumbling into me.

"I'm going for the lyre!" I called to my friends. "Cover me —"

Loki swung around, his icy claws slicing.

Jon narrowly missed getting his head knocked off. I dived over Loki's coiling tail and slid across the floor toward the lyre. Loki slammed his foot on the lyre, then thrust the Crystal Rune at the throne like a missile shot.

"No!" I cried. I couldn't reach the lyre with my hands. The only way to make a sound was to strike the strings with the sword.

I slammed the sword down.

Blanngggg! The lyre's strings snapped.

Loki arched back suddenly, then stopped.

Everything stopped.

In that moment, Loki's face was twisted to one side. I saw the venom frozen in his eyes. I had stopped time, but my head rang like a bell that Thor was pounding with his hammer. Strangely, my body kept moving. I couldn't tell you how, but I was up on my legs and jerking the point of my sword up into the ice dragon's chest.

My sword blade went up, up, up, as if I were popping a balloon with a toothpick, except the sword was sharp and heavy and real, Loki was no balloon, and my brain was threatening to explode. Up went the blade, and — *CRACK!* — with the shattering of Loki's icy hide, time roared back.

The ice dragon swooped down, and somehow I was against the underside of his chest, pushing the blade upward. Then I felt the pressure of hands pushing on my shoulders and back. Sydney and Jon were behind me, pushing me forward, holding me up.

Clank! The Crystal Rune dropped to the floor at the foot of Odin's throne. The sword was deep in

Loki's chest, and I dropped my hands just as ice crystals exploded in my face and scattered across the stone floor.

When I fell, my sword dropped to the stairs with a clang. I snatched up the broken lyre and the rune in a single grab.

A howl came from the mound of ice chunks. The dragon was no more, and Loki appeared in its place, screaming and squirming and clutching his chest with both hands.

"We did it," I said, watching Loki gasp for breath. "*We did it!*"

I pulled Jon and Sydney to their feet. We strode to the high walls. Jon held up Loki's helmet, and Sydney held the Crystal Rune. I held the lyre together with my hands and plucked one string as loudly as I could. Everything quieted for a moment as all eyes turned toward us.

In the next instant, Loki's monsters let loose a wail that reached the sky. Without Loki's powerful runic magic binding them to him, they could no longer fight. Odin and the lords and beasts of the Babylonian,

Greek, and Egyptian Underworlds quickly circled Loki's armies in a death grip, pressing them to the shore and back onto their ships.

Before we knew it, Odin and Thor burst into Valhalla. "Imprison the fiend!" Odin boomed.

Thor smashed right and left, hammering columns into jagged bars and surrounding the wounded Loki behind them, like a zoo exhibit. Spitting and growling, Loki changed into a dozen different shapes, but no matter how strong or how small, he couldn't escape his new prison. To make it that much worse, the gods set a viper over the cage to drip its venom on Loki constantly.

Drip . . . drip . . . drip . . .

"You will stay there until the *real* Ragnarok comes," Odin proclaimed. "Loki, give the order now to release Dana and her parents!"

Loki gazed up between the bars with glassy, wicked eyes. "Wait for it . . ."

"Fenrir has escaped!" cried Miss Hilda, circling overhead on her flying horse.

"And there it is!" Loki gargled a laugh. "My faithful servant makes his way to Niflheim, to execute one last command!"

"Dana!" I cried, seeing her face in my mind's eye. "Odin, we need to get to Niflheim now!"

I wasn't a hero. I was just a person with a friend. I had to bring Dana home. I wouldn't go home without her or her parents. That was all there was to it. I wouldn't go home. *We* wouldn't go home.

"Odin," I said, "please —"

Odin turned to the sea and raised his sword high. With that, Baldur's longship was dragged to shore. It was a slender boat built entirely of pine, with a single trunk, tall and straight and smooth as iron, as its mast.

"To go across the Sea of Asgard, beyond the rocks to the land of the dead, there is only one way," Odin said gravely, pointing to his son's funeral ship. "That way."

CHAPTER EIGHT

THE JOURNEY OF THE DEAD . . . AND US

Jon narrowed his eyes at Odin. "Say that again?"

But it was all too clear what Odin meant as we joined him, Thor, and the others, carrying Baldur's body down to the water.

"We're going to ride Baldur's ship to Niflheim," I said, "because that's where Dana is."

The gods rested Baldur on a platform beneath the mast. Thor laid a shroud on his brother and set the fallen god's sword and shield over it. The Valkyries piled bread and fruit by his side and stacked firewood around the platform.

With solemn faces, the gods lowered torches to the firewood. The planks began to smoke and burn.

Jon seemed to search everyone's face for a sign that this was some kind of joke. "Is everyone nuts? This may be the mythological world, but that's real fire," he said. "Don't get me wrong. I love sailing. But ride a burning ship? I don't think so —"

Even though my legs barely held me up, I walked the plank onto the deck. "I'll use the lyre to keep the flames away from us," I said. "We're going. Dana's down there. Is everybody ready?"

Ready or not, Jon and Sydney joined me on deck. With a great heave, Thor and Odin and a dozen others pushed the ship away from shore.

"You helped us today," said Odin. "May good fortune and luck be your guides!"

I would have liked a dozen extra-large gods to be our guides, but I guess when *they* went to Niflheim it was a one-way journey. As the ship floated free on the water, we quickly squirreled ourselves behind the arched prow, where I began plucking one string of the lyre, then a second, then a third until the flames leaned away from us.

The waves drew us quickly across the Sea of Asgard toward a range of distant rocks, where there was a narrow pass to the oceans beyond.

I kept playing the lyre to slow the fire's progress, and it was working. Even though the flames roared up in a ring around Baldur, his body was untouched. His face, visible above the shroud, appeared as friendly and alive as the first time we saw him.

And there was a reason for that.

"A little hot, isn't it?" Baldur sat straight up, saw the flames, and screamed. "Ahhhhhh!"

Jon and Sydney screamed, too. "Ahhhhhh!"

I quickly changed the lyre's melody, and the flames went out in a puff of gray smoke.

"What?" I gasped. "Baldur! How?"

Sydney frowned. "Maybe because it wasn't Ragnarok, after all? So Baldur couldn't die?"

Baldur laughed, then tugged the sprig of mistletoe from his neck, sniffed it, and tossed it overboard.

"Well, it's a good thing you put that fire out," he said. He noticed that we were approaching the distant rocks, and his face twisted. "Oh. I guess I know where we're going. . . ."

The wind picked up, and the waves began to push the ship toward the narrow opening in a range of cliffs that separated the Sea of Asgard from the wide oceans beyond.

"Hold on," said Jon, standing at the prow. "The space between those rocks is pretty tight. I might be able to steer us between them. Only please tell me the Norse myths don't have rocks like the Greek myths do, where they crash together and destroy all the ships going between them. Tell me."

Sydney looked up from Dana's book at Baldur. "Uh . . ."

Baldur looked from Sydney to the rocks. "Uh . . ."

Jon groaned. "You're kidding me!"

The sound of clashing stone was like a thunderclap as the great black cliffs unhinged and struck each other, sending an avalanche of shattered rock into the sea. Before we could do anything to stop them, the rocks pulled apart, and the current sucked our ship toward them.

"I've got it!" Baldur shouted, grabbing hold of the rudder. "Just a twist and a turn and a —"

Sydney grabbed my arm. "Look there! On the cliffs!" A thin figure dressed in black from head to foot bounded from rock to rock above us. It was clearly a man. He ducked when the waves washed up, and then made his way, ledge by ledge, to the water's edge.

"We've seen a guy like that before," said Jon. "It looks like . . ." His jaw fell open. "Wait a second . . . the stranger at the museum?"

"The thief?" said Sydney. "The stranger who's after the lyre!"

In a flash it came back to me — the shadowy figure, skulking through the halls of the art museum the night we plotted to steal the Lyre of Orpheus.

"Hey!" I shouted up at him.

The man stopped on a ledge. He raised his right hand high. Then he raised his fingers, first four of them, then two, then three, and finally one.

"Who are you?" I called out. "What do you want?"

But the man simply repeated what he did with his fingers. Four, two, three, one.

We lost sight of him as the ship spun forward.

"Get ready to row!" said Baldur as the prow nosed between the rocks. "If I wasn't dead before, I may be soon!" I hoped he was just kidding, but we huddled over the oars as he weaved the ship from side to side, slowing its forward motion until the rocks were as far apart as they could be. "And — row!" We plunged the oars into the water and pulled hard. The water threw us between and past the rocks with inches to spare before they crashed together with a deep *BOOM*.

"Yeah, Baldur!" whooped Jon.

But it wasn't any better on the other side. We bobbed wildly away from Asgard on heaving seas. Over the tops of the waves, we could see plumes of black smoke rising from the distant shorelines in every direction.

"Your world?" said Baldur.

"Oh, man. It's worse than before," said Sydney. "So many fires."

Suddenly, the surface of the sea exploded, and an enormous serpent raised its head.

"The Midgard Serpent!" Baldur shouted. "Another one of Loki's ugly children! Jon, hold the rudder with me!"

The serpent, a huge thing covered with black scales and streaky red spikes, roared and slapped its tail hard, sending a giant wave toward us. Jon jumped to the back of the ship and helped Baldur steer us directly into the wave. The ship spun around and around. Somehow, we lost sight of the serpent and found ourselves sailing down a familiar coast.

I don't know how, but the boat had brought us to Pinewood Bluffs.

"Whoa!" Jon breathed. "Look at the smoke."

I wanted so much to stop, to see my family. But my family wasn't there. They had gone with everyone else when the town was evacuated.

And there was no going anywhere but Niflheim. Dana was still missing.

"There's Power Island," said Sydney, pointing up ahead, "where we fought the Cyclopes. One of the entrances to the Norse Underworld is somewhere beneath it, remember?"

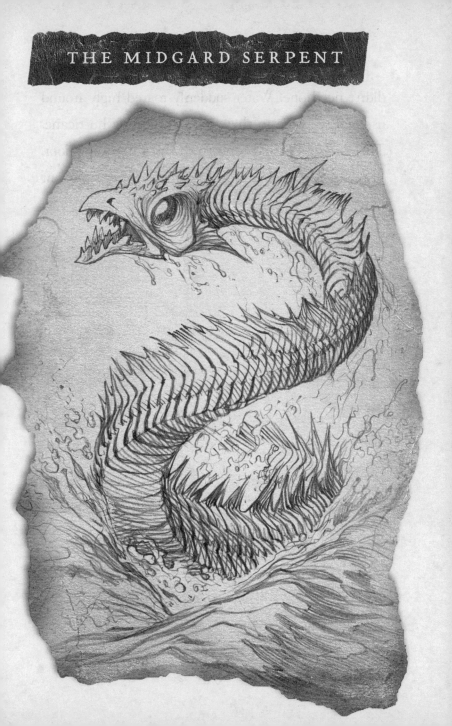

I had no clue how we'd find it, but apparently I didn't need one. Water suddenly roared high around us, as if we were in the eye of a spinning hurricane. The black sea parted beneath the boat like a trapdoor. We hung in the air for a moment, screaming our lungs out.

Then we fell.

CHAPTER NINE

A REALLY UGLY CASTLE

"HOLD TIGHT TO — SOMETHING!" I CRIED.

With the ship in free fall, we jumped on one another like football players in a pileup and clung to the rigging, while Baldur peered over the side. "Uh-oh —"

"What?" I said.

WHUMP! The ship hit water hard, then rushed forward like a racing boat.

"There's no controlling it now!" Baldur yelled. "Hold on!"

The ship roared along a white-capped river until we were thrown into another waterway, then another and another. I counted eleven rivers in all, each faster than the one before, until we were dumped into a narrow channel jammed with ice floes.

"What just happened?" asked Sydney, climbing to her feet and looking a little green.

"Whatever it was," said Jon, wobbling next to her, "I hope it never happens again."

The boat slowed to a crawl as the icy river narrowed even more.

"Niflheim," said Baldur gravely. "The smell of death gives it away."

I wasn't sure what death smelled like, but the air was thick with the odor of something rotting, and barely breathable. Poor Dana. I so wanted to get her out of there.

The lyre in my lap was barely in one piece, but I used the time to try to restring it. I couldn't help thinking about Orpheus' journey to the Greek

Underworld to rescue his new wife. After everything he did, charming the beasts and even Hades himself, he couldn't save her. It wasn't meant to be.

I imagined how horrible he must have felt, knowing he had tried everything and still failed. We needed to do better . . . but the lyre in my hands was so fragile now. I remembered the mysterious man climbing the rocks and signaling to us. Could he really be the same person as at the museum? Did he want the lyre, too?

And what did he mean — four, two, three, one?

Jon tugged my sleeve. "Time's up."

I reattached and tightened the lyre's last string as best I could, then looked up. We were drifting toward a long wooden pier jutting out from the riverbank. Lanterns on the pier cast a sick green light on the black water. Beyond the pier stood a bridge with a gold roof.

"The port of the dead," said Sydney, reading from Dana's notes.

"It is," whispered Baldur. "And that's the infamous Gjoll Bridge. The gold roof is made of the shields of the dead whose souls were not chosen by my sisters to join Odin. Not many of the living have ever seen it. This is Niflheim."

The bridge was frightening in its own way, but nothing like the immensity in the distance behind it. There was a tree whose trunk must have measured miles from side to side. It reached to a height far beyond anything I could see.

"The giant ash tree is the axis of all three worlds," said Baldur. "Niflheim, Midgard, and Asgard."

I tried to imagine how everything was connected to everything else. Norse mythology was one thing, but how did all the other branches of mythology fit in? It was all too much. Besides, I had plenty of other things to worry about.

As our ship mysteriously drifted to the pier, a troop of ghostly Draugs emerged from the darkness in a slow procession. They carried a portable platform — and I knew right away what it was for.

"Uh-oh," I said. "They're coming for you, Baldur."

He grumbled under his breath. "To get into the castle, we must fool the keepers of the dead," he whispered. "It seems a shame to let my funeral go to waste.

I'll play dead. You should, too. Everyone, quietly, get under my shroud!" Baldur lay flat on the funeral platform and pulled the heavy cloth over him. Without any other option, we ducked underneath and clung to the underside of the platform. "Psst," Baldur said. "When we get inside the castle, you three sneak off to find Dana. I'll play dead until the Draugs get wise. Now, shhh!"

Frozen in place, we heard the grumbling of the ghostly Draug warriors walking down the pier toward the ship. They smelled bad, as usual, but there was another smell on them we all recognized — the sour stink of Fenrir. He was definitely in Niflheim.

We were carried inland to where the ground was mostly frozen swamp, black with stubbly growth. The Draugs marched silently past all kinds of wailing, which I figured must have been coming from souls of the dead. They were angry, or sad, or both.

But it was about to get worse.

The Draugs paused, set down the platform, and strode away. I lifted the shroud for a moment to peek out. We were alone.

"There," Sydney whispered. A huge, ugly building made of mismatched iron, stone, and wood rose up on a hill in front of the giant tree.

"I bet Dana's in there," I said. "Her parents, too. They have to be."

"There's supposed to be a monster dog, Garm, guarding Niflheim's fortress," Baldur whispered. "I don't sense him nearby."

"Maybe he's being walked by . . . what's Loki's daughter's name?" Jon asked.

"Hela," I said, shivering a little. "Dana told me once. It's a name you don't forget."

Clang! The chains fell and the gate squealed open. After a minute, the Draugs hauled us across the threshold.

The Draugs set us down again so they could close the gate behind them. That's when Baldur whispered, "Now!" We slipped out from under the shroud and darted into the shadows. I wished Baldur a silent "good luck." We would all need it.

Hela's fortress was a city of pointed arches and tall pinnacles, stone bridges and cobbled streets. There were narrow passageways everywhere, low-roofed houses, and plumes of smoke rising from what looked like shops, though I couldn't imagine what they sold there. In the middle of the city stood a crazy structure made of crumbling stone and rotting wooden beams piled up to impossible heights. It was surrounded by a bad-smelling swamp of black reeds and vines.

Sydney breathed out. "If I was keeping people prisoner, which I would never do, that ugly place is where I'd put them. Dana and her parents must be in there."

I plucked the strings of the lyre one by one. They barely made a ripple, but the magical sound rolled back the dense sludge just enough to give us a path to the gate.

Unfortunately, the creepy guard dog must have returned from his walk, because there he was. He was huge, a big black-haired monster on four legs with a head just a little smaller than an oil drum.

"Well, he's ugly," said Jon. "Along with everything else here."

"According to the myths, Garm has one purpose,"

said Sydney. "He guards the Niflheim fortress. That's all he does."

Garm fixed us with his bright red eyes and stepped forward. We shrank back.

I pulled out the lyre again.

"Plus, he's deaf," she added.

I holstered the lyre and drew my sword.

Garm growled like rumbling thunder.

"I think we're going to have to fight," I said. "Again."

"Maybe not," said Jon. "Even crazy monster dogs get hungry, don't they?" He dug into a pocket and pulled out a chunk of toasted bread. We blinked at him.

"What? I grabbed it when you put out the fire on the boat. I didn't think Baldur would miss it." He pulled us behind him, then tossed the bread high. This surprised Garm, and he leaped for it. We raced past him into the black hall, shutting the big door quietly behind us.

Apparently not quietly enough.

The instant we set foot on the stone floor, doors flashed open all around us, and a hundred Draug warriors rushed in.

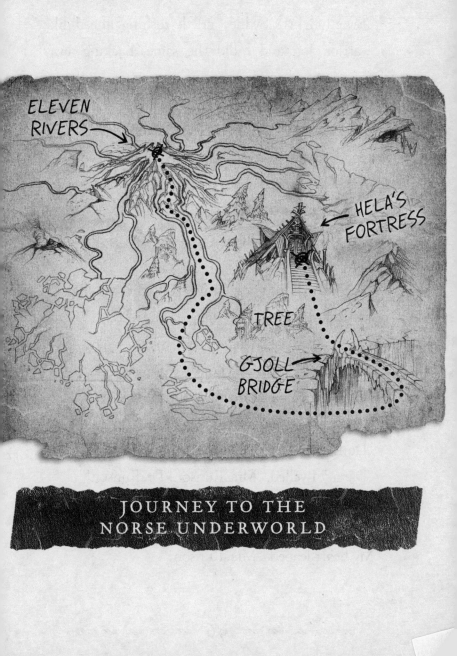

ELEVEN
RIVERS

HELA'S
FORTRESS

TREE

GJOLL
BRIDGE

JOURNEY TO THE
NORSE UNDERWORLD

"Sword fight!" Sydney cried, rushing ahead like a warrior. Jon and I did the same, hacking away with our swords and surprising the Draugs with our ferocity.

Too bad ferocity only gets you so far. The Draugs were far better sword fighters, having practiced, like, forever. They lunged. They parried. They lunged again. We mostly jumped aside.

"Back up!" Jon shouted, pointing. "Across the floor to that passage!"

We dashed into a passage so tight the Draugs couldn't follow us. They gargled a bunch of weird words, doubled back, and circled around.

"Hurry!" said Sydney. "Look —"

We squeezed out the end of the passage into a corridor of big iron doors, all chained shut.

"Dungeons, anyone?" said Jon.

"Dana!" I yelled. "Mrs. Runson! Dr. Runson!"

I clanged my sword lightly on every door until I heard an answer. "Owen Brown? Is that you?"

My heart leaped. "Mrs. Runson!"

"Stand back from the door!" Sydney raised her sword with both hands and brought the blade down on the door latch. The blow dented it, but her sword bounced back and nearly struck her in the helmet.

"My turn!" said Jon.

We took turns. *Clang! Clang! Clang!* Together, the three of us finally hacked the latch to pieces. The door swung open, and Dr. and Mrs. Runson rushed out. "We never believed . . ."

"Where's Dana?" I said, scanning the empty cell behind them.

They looked at each other. Mrs. Runson buried her face in her hands. Dr. Runson shook his head. "Hela has her," he said softly. "She refuses to let her go."

All at once, the door at the end of the passage burst open, and the whole place lit up like a city at night. The passage swarmed with the same angry Draugs as before, and Garm, too.

But we hardly looked at them.

Because out of the midst of the dead Viking warriors stepped . . . an even deader person. A demon . . . a witch . . . a corpse.

I knew exactly who it was — Loki's evil daughter, Hela.

"And now . . . I have you all!" she crowed.

Hela was quite a sight, to say the least. She was an old skull-headed lady with stringy white hair. Her hands were the bones of a skeleton, hanging together with stringy sinews. Her arms and legs, visible under her cloak — *ugh!* — were covered in rags that may or may not have been rotten flesh. When she cracked open her jaws, worms slithered out.

She was a nice lady.

Oh, and on her skull-head sat a crown of mangled metal that looked as if it was left over from a really bad car crash.

I cleared my throat. "We've come for Dana."

"She cannot leave my Underworld," Hela said. Her voice was as cracked and rusty as her crown. "Fenrir came with my father's command. The girl stays. You . . . may go."

It escapes me how a dead skeleton lady could have breath, but she did, and it was really stinky. I nearly fainted. "We're not leaving without her." I stepped forward, my sword raised.

The Runsons, who probably knew enough to keep quiet, poked fingers in my shoulders. "Careful," they whispered. "She's a goddess, and really powerful."

Hela jerked her way around us like a puppet on wires. It was sickening.

"Suit yourself," she said. "Fenrir will make sure you stay with your friend. Of course, you have to be dead to really fit in." She grinned wickedly. "But the Draugs and Garm will happily oblige."

"At least let us see Dana," said Dr. Runson. "We have to see our daughter."

Hela laughed so loudly that a whole crew of worms dribbled down her chin. "Fenrir took her to his lair! She's at the center of a maze of glass so intricate only Fenrir himself can thread his way in and out. I can't get in if I wanted to. No, Dana Runson is lost to you. So go! Before I lose my patience and keep you all —"

Mrs. Runson began to cry.

I plucked the lyre softly, playing over the strings to see what worked on Hela.

"Stop that noise," she said calmly. "It grates on me, and doesn't do anything except make me angrier."

So I stopped. Still, I had to get her to make a deal. Too bad I didn't think it through before I opened my mouth.

"I'll go to Fenrir's lair," I said. "I'll vanquish him. I'll bring Dana out."

"What?" said Jon. "Owen, that's —"

Hela whipped her ugly face around to me. "Oh, you will? You can't possibly succeed at any of those things."

My heart pounded like a jackhammer. "I will. And if I come back with Dana . . . ?"

Hela was silent for a while. "Then you may take her home. But —"

"Here it comes," said Sydney.

"You think yourself a junior Orpheus?" Hela said darkly. "Then find your way to Fenrir's lair. Vanquish him if you can. Bring Dana back with you. But if you look back at her, for even a second, for a fraction of a second, she remains in Niflheim forever . . . *and so do you.* Deal?"

I felt like my head was stuffed with wool. I had no choice. "Deal."

Hela roared with tinny laughter. "Then follow me, everyone! To the mouth of Fenrir's maze. Let's watch as this boy fails!"

CHAPTER TEN

THE MYTH OF ORPHEUS

AS WE TRAMPED DEEPER INTO HELA'S CASTLE THAN we ever wanted to go, I turned to my friends. "Dr. Runson, Mrs. Runson, tell me what you know about Orpheus. Sydney, read me everything you can find in Dana's book!"

Down every set of stairs, down every ramp, the Runsons talked, Sydney read, and Jon patted my shoulders over and over until my brain was mush.

Was I Orpheus? No. Could I do anything at all like he did? Who knew? He was strong. He was a hero of the journey of the Argonauts. A hero in the Quest for the Golden Fleece. A hero — until he failed to rescue his wife from Hades.

Who was I?

Owen Brown. A kid.

"And here we are!" Hela rasped, fluttering her ragged robes around.

What we were looking at was a series of glass walls, ten or twelve feet tall. They were angled this way and that, and their edges looked as sharp as razor blades. Far away, in what I guessed was the center of the maze, we could make out the shape of a beast with red fur — Fenrir — pacing back and forth. Every few seconds, we glimpsed a figure behind him, standing motionless. Dana.

The Runsons hugged each other close.

Hela turned her beady eyes on me. "I have all the time in the world. But I don't think she does. Your move."

"Owen," said Sydney quietly, patting my arm.

"I know," I said.

"Good luck," said Mrs. Runson.

"Thanks."

I looked at Jon. He just nodded. I nodded back.

And I entered the maze.

It was as if I had entered another world.

The glass walls were as sharp as they looked, which I found out when I glanced back at everyone, and they watched me walk straight into one wall, bounce off another wall, and slide to the floor, nearly slicing myself in two.

"Careful!" I yelped to myself.

I rose to my feet slowly. But there were so many corridors, and at such crazy angles, that all I saw were reflections of myself. Dana and the center weren't getting an inch closer.

Then I remembered for the second time that day what I'd learned so painfully in the Babylonian Underworld. Spaces resonated with a particular sound, a single pitch all their own. If I could play the right notes, the lyre might be able to help me make my way between the glass walls to Dana.

I'd think about my inevitable battle with Fenrir when I got there. If I got there. No, *when* I got there. Part of being a hero was having confidence in yourself, right?

Bling . . . boong . . . pling-g-g-g!

The wall ahead of me resounded as I plucked the lyre. The sound echoed from one wall to another, all the way around what I guessed was a hidden corner. I slipped around it, played more notes, and a farther wall echoed. I moved to it, found a passage that was otherwise invisible, and played the lyre again. Note by note, step-by-step, I made my way to the center of the maze.

And Dana.

And Fenrir.

Dana was as excited to see me as I was to see her.

Fenrir, not so much.

He growled, and the smell of his breath almost knocked me over. His venom dripped and hissed on the ground. If giant wolves could smile, I was sure Fenrir was smiling now, as if he saw his supper. My brain flashed with everything all at once. The first time I'd seen Fenrir at Dana's house. The museum where Jon, Sydney, and I stole the lyre. The stranger at the museum whom we might have just seen in Asgard.

Then all the pieces fell into place. And I laughed.

"Really, Owen?" said Dana. "Laughing at a time like this?"

"The stranger," I said. "He didn't follow us at all. He followed the lyre."

And suddenly I knew exactly what he meant by that riddle: four, two, three, one.

Fenrir growled and prepared to leap at me. Before he could, I played those notes: four, two, three, one. All at once, his back arched up like an angry cat's, and he sank to the floor at my feet. Then he shrank into the back corner of his lair. He curled up, tucked his ugly head between his front paws . . . and started to whimper.

"Owen Brown!" came a distant yell that I recognized as Hela's. "Remember our deal!"

I kept playing the lyre notes so that Fenrir would stay where he was, and filled Dana in.

Her eyes narrowed. "Owen, that is so dumb!" she cried.

"Believe me, I know," I said. "But that's the deal. Ready? Here we go."

I turned my back on her. We started out of the core of the maze, me in the lead, Dana following. I played the lyre — four, two, three, one — and took the turns, left, right, to the side, backward, straight ahead. We were making our way out. Well, I was making my way out. I couldn't hear Dana.

Orpheus couldn't stop himself from looking back to see if his wife was still behind him, and I knew why. He must have felt just like I felt. I wanted to know that Dana was there. In this place, crafted by Loki, the trickster god himself, how could anyone be sure that the whole thing wasn't a horrible trick? For all I knew, the whole journey might still be a colossal failure. Then we'd be living out our days in Niflheim forever.

And yet, note by note, we got closer to the entrance.

Five more turns in the maze, and we would be out. Or maybe only I would be out. Looking through the glass walls, I saw Jon, Sydney, and the Runsons. I looked at their eyes. They stared at me, then they searched the maze behind me. What was in their faces? Did they see Dana behind me? Or was I alone? I couldn't tell.

Then I knew I had to look. I had to see if this was a trick. . . .

My neck twitched. I felt my muscles straining, trying to hold my head forward. My heart pounded. My head ached. I heard nothing behind me. She wasn't there. *She wasn't there!*

I opened my lips. I breathed in. My head turned to the side.

No!

I rushed ahead, playing the last note loud and full, and I was out of the maze.

Everyone screamed.

And Dana was there, clutching at my shoulders, pulling me to the ground, collapsing on me. Everyone piled on top of us.

Hela shrieked like a banshee. "Nooooo! Draugs — kill — them — all!"

Then, before we knew what was happening, Hela hurtled through the air and came down hard in the middle of the Draugs, knocking them all down like bowling pins.

"What?" I gasped.

And there was Baldur, dusting his hands together. "Hela's heavier than she looks! I didn't come too early, did I?"

"Right on time!" shouted Sydney.

"Then let's get out of here," Baldur said. "My ship makes return trips, you know!"

In a flash of speed, we sprinted back through the passage, up and down stairs, and out the castle gate. We scrambled onto the ship, and pushed off into the crazy sequence of rivers that brought us there, all before Hela and her Draugs could catch us.

"Up the eleven rivers — to home!" Jon yelled.

My heart was in my throat. I held on to Dana as if my life depended on it, and she held on to Sydney and Jon. The Runsons clung to Baldur and screamed the whole way back. We flew from river to river, up into our own world. Pinewood Bluffs still smoked and smoldered. But our journey wasn't over. We slid through the black rocks as easily as the first time, and Asgard was in view now, its fields peaceful, its shore teeming with heroes.

"There it is!" cried Mrs. Runson, clutching her husband tight. "I can't believe we're actually seeing it."

As the ship approached, Odin and Thor came running to the shore. The ship docked and we set foot on solid ground. The huge field of gods and heroes gave out a thunderous cheer that seemed to last forever.

"I live!" said Baldur, and Odin, Thor, and the Valkyries all embraced him.

"My son is alive!" Odin boomed. "Children, you have my eternal allegiance. The bells of doom shall not ring today. Tomorrow and tomorrow and tomorrow will come!"

"Owen, look," Dana whispered, pointing out a hooded figure dressed in black racing across the rainbow bridge toward us.

"The stranger," I said.

The man ran up the hill directly to us. He wasn't large, not built like a god, though I knew he was half-god. Breathing hard, he pulled back his hood with slender fingers to reveal a sad but kind face, a mop of brown hair, and a garland of sharp-edged leaves banding his forehead.

Hades, as large as he was, bowed before the thin man. "And it comes full circle."

"Allow me, Owen Brown," said the man. "I believe what you are holding belongs to me. I am Orpheus."

I knew it.

The Runsons gasped. Dana clutched my arm. Jon's and Sydney's jaws fell open. My knees buckled under me. Luckily, Baldur was there to hold me up.

I bowed and held out the lyre. "Orpheus, I'm sorry. I had to . . . sort of . . . chop it in half."

Surprisingly, Orpheus smiled when he took the pieces of the lyre into his hands. "You'll have to do a lot more damage to stop this thing." With a quick flash of his fingers, he restored the lyre to its original shape, playing all seven strings brightly as if they were brand-new. "You play it well. We all thank you."

ORPHEUS

Odin nodded slowly. "An instrument of great magic," he said. "And perhaps, having it back again, Orpheus, you can do something to stop the Fires of Midgard?"

"My pleasure," said Orpheus, looking up at the great god. "But maybe we can do this . . . together?"

So together, Orpheus and Odin wafted the last clouds of battle away, and we could see all the way beyond the Sea of Asgard to our own world, where snow was falling heavily.

"Snow!" said Odin, happier than we'd seen him yet.

"Snow on snow on snow will drown the Midgard fires!" added Orpheus.

After saying our good-byes, Kingu, Ullikummi, and his armies left as they had come. Anubis and his canine warriors departed after a long, low bow. So did Hades and his heroes, who turned toward the distant hills and marched away. Orpheus waved once to us, then marched along with his countrymen, playing triumphant songs.

"Midgard will rebuild," said Thor, beaming down at

us. "We shall watch you. Your services will never be forgotten."

Odin thanked us last of all. "You children — you *heroes* — have staved off our final day, now that he is vanquished." He gestured to Valhalla, where Loki lay imprisoned in his poisonous cell. "Tomorrow will come, after all. Thank you . . . forever!"

The journey home was the same as the journey to Asgard, on the Valkyries' flying horses, and it was just as fast. The snowflakes fell like gentle rain until the fires in Pinewood Bluffs finally went out. The destruction was shocking, but not as bad as I had feared.

Pinewood Bluffs was calm when the Valkyries landed on the front lawn of the Runsons' house.

"So, will you still be our lunch ladies?" Sydney asked.

"Oh, yes," said Miss Lillian. "The pay is good, we get free meals, and Odin wants us to stay near. Your school being so close to the Underworlds has its advantages. You never know. Anything could happen."

"And probably will," said Miss Marge flatly.

I didn't know whether to feel good about that, or terrified. It was like wondering what Monday's chef's surprise would be.

Once inside, Dr. and Mrs. Runson called our parents and learned that they were driving back, after having evacuated from town. They were overjoyed to hear that we were all safe. The Runsons invited us to stay at their house until our parents returned.

It was all over. The world didn't end, and that was pretty much the best thing ever.

Really, it was.

But standing there, looking over the town, thinking back over the whole thing, I felt a little . . . empty. Maybe it was the letdown at the end of the adventure. An adventure that, as dangerous and unbelievable as it had been, was pretty thrilling.

After everything, I was just Owen Brown again.

Student at Pinewood Bluffs Elementary.

Friend of Jon, Sydney, and Dana.

Brother of Mags.

We got the furnace going, and Mrs. Runson set up a fire in the fireplace. It would be hours before our folks were back, so Mrs. and Dr. Runson went into the kitchen to rustle up something for dinner.

Dana, Jon, Sydney, and I sat on the couch, watching the snow pile up outside the windows. It was a little early in the season for snow, but because it helped put out the fires, no one was complaining. Also, Orpheus and Odin's snow must have had a magical element of forgetfulness, because nobody was yelling about monsters or men in silver armor. They'd probably just chalked the fires up to a dry spell and wind. That was fine with me. No one needed to know that the world had nearly ended.

Life was mostly normal again. Or as normal as it would ever be, with an entrance to the Underworlds under our school.

"Do you think we'll have classes tomorrow?" I asked, peering out at the snow.

"I hope so," said Sydney. "After the last few days, I wouldn't mind a nice, boring quiz or two. Besides, remember what Odin said? Tomorrow will come, after all."

Jon nodded. "Hey, tomorrow is Monday. I wonder what the lunch ladies have planned for the chef's surprise!"

That's when we pummeled Jon with pillows.

GLOSSARY

Anubis (Egyptian Mythology): the jackal-headed god responsible for mummification and the afterlife

Asgard (Norse Mythology): home of the Norse gods and the court of Odin

Baldur (Norse Mythology): Norse god and son of Odin

Fenrir (Norse Mythology): a giant, fire-breathing red wolf

Hades (Greek Mythology): the ruler of the Greek Underworld

Hela (Norse Mythology): daughter of Loki and goddess of the Norse Underworld

Kingu (Babylonian Mythology): a famous Babylonian warrior who rebelled against Marduk and was cursed with the body of a scorpion

Loki (Norse Mythology): a trickster god

Lyre of Orpheus (Greek Mythology): a stringed instrument that charms people, animals, and objects into doing things for Orpheus

Midgard (Norse Mythology): a name for the world of humans

Niflheim (Norse Mythology): the Underworld of Norse myth

Orpheus (Greek Mythology): a musician who traveled to the Underworld to bring his wife back from the dead

Ragnarok (Norse Mythology): the twilight of the gods and the end of Norse divinity

Runes (Norse Mythology): old, powerful stones with magic symbols carved on them

Thor (Norse Mythology): a hammer-wielding god and son of Odin, often associated with thunder

Valhalla (Norse Mythology): the large, majestic hall of the gods located in Asgard and ruled over by Odin

Valkyries (Norse Mythology): women who work for Odin and choose who lives and dies in battle

THE SECRETS OF DROON

By Tony Abbott

An epic journey—and an incredible series!

Read them all!

◢ SCHOLASTIC

www.scholastic.com/droon

DROON36-8

THE DARK REALM

NIXA THE DEATH BRINGER

EQUINUS THE SPIRIT HORSE

RASHOUK THE CAVE TROLL

FIGHT THE BEASTS

LUNA THE MOON WOLF

BLAZE THE ICE DRAGON

STEALTH THE GHOST PANTHER

FEAR THE MAGIC